This book ~~belongs to~~ is controlled by

_____

ESCAPE | POWER

For Mandy

Henry Holt and Company, LLC
Publishers since 1866
175 Fifth Avenue
New York, New York 10010
mackids.com

Library of Congress Cataloging-in-Publication Data is available.
ISBN 978-1-62779-933-1

Our books may be purchased in bulk for promotional, educational, or
business use. Please contact your local bookseller or the Macmillan
Corporate and Premium Sales Department at (800) 221-7945 ext. 5442
or by e-mail at MacmillanSpecialMarkets@macmillan.com.

First published in the United Kingdom in 2016 by Oxford University Press
First American edition—2016

Printed in China by Leo Paper Group, Gulao Town, Heshan,
Guangdong Province

10 9 8 7 6 5 4 3 2 1

This book is out of control!

Richard BYRNE

Henry Holt and Company · New York

Bella was at home when someone on the other page knocked at the door.

It was Ben.
He had a new toy to show Bella.

"It's remote controlled," said Ben. "Watch what the ladder does when I press the **UP** button."

But nothing seemed to happen.
So Ben pressed the SPIN **button.**

"It's just not moving!" said Bella.
"See if it will make a noise instead."
So Ben pressed the SIREN button.

WOO-WOO!

"It's a bit quiet," said Bella.
"Try a different noise.
How about the VOICE button?"

"Who said that?"
asked Bella.

"It's your dog!
He's talking!"
said Ben.

But it didn't!

"Oops!"
said Ben.

Bella thought for a moment.
"Dear reader," she began. . . .

"Can you
help us?

Please press the
DOWN button!"

Oh dear.
That didn't work.

Ben was starting
to feel a little
queasy.

"Quick!" he said.
"Try the **ESCAPE** button."

But things became even more muddled.

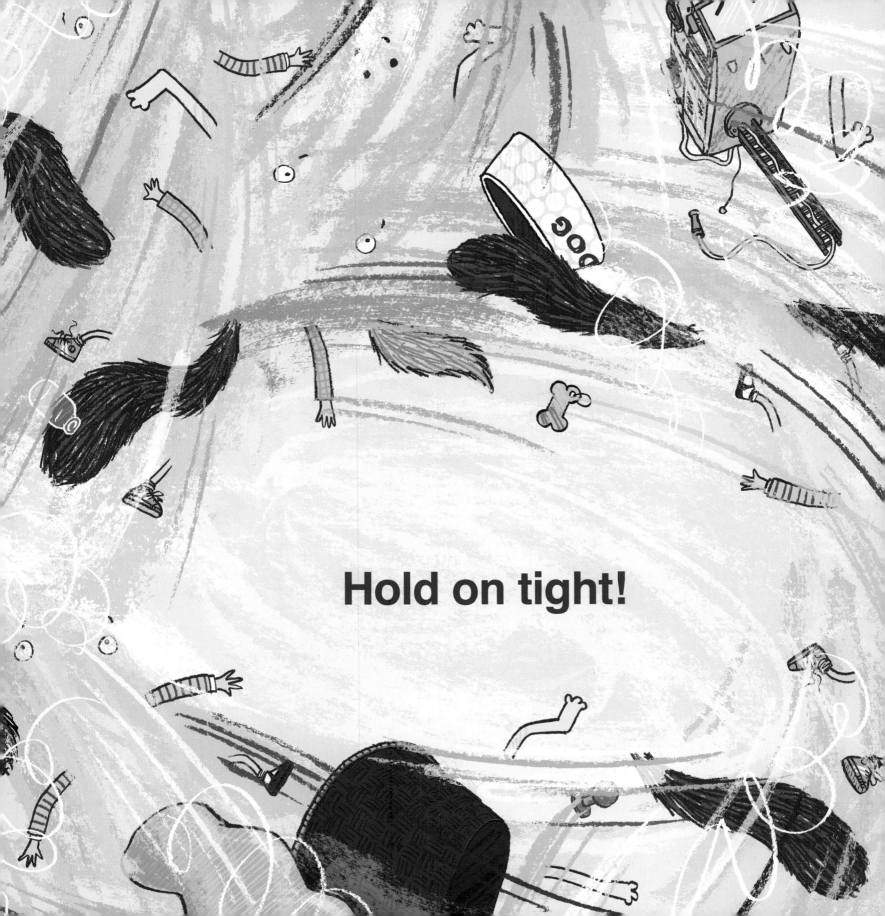

Hold on tight!

But suddenly, everything was back under control. Phew! Bella's dog clicked a button . . .

and the ladder went up!

Then he pressed a different button . . .

and the water came down. "Naughty dog," said Bella.